MW00769304

# Hello Cocky!

**Aimee Aryal**

**Illustrated by Joni Graybill**
University of South Carolina, Class of 2005

www.mascotbooks.com

It was a beautiful fall day at the
University of South Carolina.

Cocky was on his way to
Williams-Brice Stadium to watch
a football game.

He walked around the Horseshoe
and stopped in front of
McKissick Museum.

Dr. Sorensen, the President of the
University of South Carolina, said,
"Hello Cocky!"

Cocky passed by Russell House.

Some students standing outside
waved, "Hello Cocky!"

Cocky walked over to
Thomas-Cooper Library.

A professor passing by said,
"Hello Cocky!"

Cocky stopped at the Carolina Center
where the Gamecocks
play basketball.

A group of USC fans standing nearby
shouted, "Hello Cocky!"

It was almost time for the football game.
As Cocky walked to the stadium,
he passed by some alumni.

The alumni remembered Cocky
from when they went to USC.
They said, "Hello, again, Cocky!"

Finally, Cocky arrived at the stadium.

As he ran onto the football field,
the crowd cheered,
"Let's Go Gamecocks!"

Cocky watched the game from
the sidelines and cheered for the team.

The Gamecocks scored six points!
The quarterback shouted,
"Touchdown Cocky!"

At half-time the Carolina Marching Band performed on the field.

Cocky and the crowd listened to
"The Fighting Gamecocks Lead the Way."

The South Carolina Fighting Gamecocks
won the football game!

Cocky gave Coach Holtz
a high-five. The coach said,
"Great game Cocky!"

After the football game, Cocky was tired. It had been a long day at the University of South Carolina.

He walked home and climbed into bed.

"Goodnight Cocky."

For Anna and Maya, and
all of Cocky's little fans. ~ AA

To all my family and friends
who helped me realize my dream. ~ JG

Special thanks to:

Ken Corbett

Lou Holtz

Debbie Sherer

Dr. Andrew Sorensen

For information please contact Mascot Books,
P.O. Box 220157, Chantilly, VA 20153-0157.

ISBN: 1-932888-07-1

Printed in the United States.

www.mascotbooks.com